WHAT IF...?

Anthony Browne

CANDLEWICK PRESS

Withdrawn

WHAT IF. . .?

Joe was going to his first big party.
It was at his friend Tom's house,
but Joe had lost the invitation and
didn't know the house number.

"It's OK, Joe," said Mom. "Tom lives somewhere on this street. We'll find it."
So they set off.

"No," said Joe.

"No!"
said Joe.

"NO!"
said Joe.

"NO!" said Joe.

"Can't you come earlier?" asked Joe. "What if it's awful?"

"You'll enjoy it," said Mom.

"I bet you won't want to come home."

"I bet I will," said Joe.

"Is this the house?" asked Mom.

"NO!" said Joe.

They had come to the end
of the street.

Then they saw it: Tom's house.

The door opened slowly . . .

and Joe went in.

And Mom went home.

I hope Joe will be all right. . . .
Of course he will — it's only a party!
But what if he's REALLY unhappy?

Two hours later . . .

Knock! Knock! Mom went in. . . .

"Hi, Mom! I had a GREAT time!"

"Oh, good," said Mom.

"I was wondering, Joe, if you'd like
to have a party on *your* birthday."

"YES, PLEASE!"

said Joe.

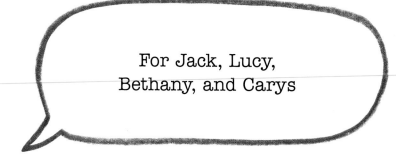

For Jack, Lucy,
Bethany, and Carys

First U.S. edition 2014

Library of Congress Catalog Card Number 2013952843
ISBN 978-0-7636-7419-9

14 15 16 17 18 19 TLF 10 9 8 7 6 5 4 3 2 1

Printed in Dongguan, Guangdong, China

This book was typeset in ITC American Typewriter and Tekton.
The illustrations were done in gouache and crayon.

Candlewick Press
99 Dover Street
Somerville, Massachusetts 02144

visit us at www.candlewick.com